For Rachel and Mia

SIMON & SCHUSTER BOOKS FOR YOUNG READERS
An imprint of Simon & Schuster Children's Publishing Division
1230 Avenue of the Americas, New York, New York 10020
Copyright © 2013 by Dan Krall
SIMON & SCHUSTER BOOKS FOR YOUNG READERS is a trademark of Simon & Schuster, Inc.
For information about special discounts for bulk purchases, please contact Simon & Schuster Special Sales at
1-866-506-1949 or business@simonandschuster.com.
The Simon & Schuster Speakers Bureau can bring authors to your live event. For more information or to book an event,
contact the Simon & Schuster Speakers Bureau at 1-866-248-3049 or visit our website at www.simonspeakers.com.
Book design by Lizzy Bromley
The text for this book is set in Optima LT Std.
The illustrations for this book are rendered in Photoshop.
Manufactured in China
0213 SCP
2 4 6 8 10 9 7 5 3 1
Library of Congress Cataloging-in-Publication Data
Krall, Dan.
The great lollipop caper / Dan Krall.
p. cm.
Summary: Tired of having only adults like his acidic taste, Mr. Caper makes caper-flavored lollipops that are sent throughout
the world, but his plot has unexpected consequences and only Lollipop can save the day.
ISBN 978-1-4424-4460-7 (hardcover : alk. paper)
ISBN 978-1-4424-4461-4 (eBook : alk. paper)
[1. Contentment—Fiction. 2. Pickles—Fiction. 3. Lollipops—Fiction. 4. Humorous stories.] I. Title.
PZ7.K85865Gre 2013
[E]—dc23 2012004041

first
edition

The Great LoLLIPOP CAPER

by

Dan Krall

SIMON & SCHUSTER BOOKS FOR YOUNG READERS

New York London Toronto Sydney New Delhi

For those of you who don't know, a caper is a tiny pickled sourpuss, who lives in a jar in your fridge and is never eaten by children.

Of course, everyone knows
what a lollipop is, which is
why Mr. Caper is so angry.

Mr. Caper never liked Lollipop.

Sure, adults admired Mr. Caper's acidic earthiness.

But Mr. Caper didn't care about adults.

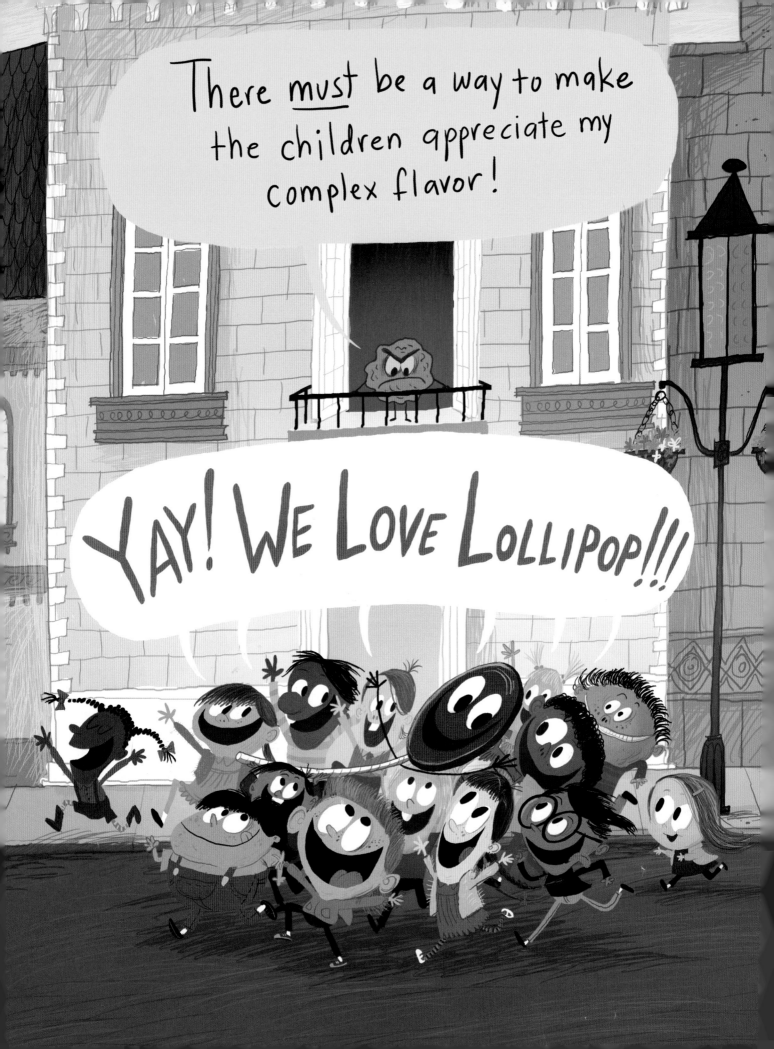

Disguised as a harmless pea,
Mr. Caper sneaks into the lollipop factory.

Soon, Mr. Caper's new flavor of lollipop was being packed up and sent all over the world.

CHINA

FRANCE

But when the children ate the new caper-flavored lollipops, something strange and unexpected happened.

They became as bitter and sour as Mr. Caper tasted.
They started acting in the most appalling ways.

why?
Mr. Caper! What have you done?!
I used to like capers.
Bad caper.
I'm very disappointed in you.

Mr. Caper's plan had backfired.

Now no one liked Mr. Caper.
He was all alone.

After one delicious taste, the children of
the world instantly changed back into their
former sweet selves. The day was saved.

Except . . .

Well, at least the children are sweet again, but now I guess I'm stuck being sour and alone.
Aw, don't be silly, Mr. Caper. Sure, those kids love me now, but when they grow up, guess who they're going to be crazy about?

We missed you, Mr. Caper!
Aww, Mr. Caper, it's okay.
We couldn't stay mad at you.

And on that day Mr. Caper learned how sweet
being earthy and acidic could be.